To Annabella,
Harmony!

David Ian Pottertleg

GWENDOLYN'S
NUTTY NUTCRACKER

Written by David Ira Rottenberg

Illustrated by Zachery Manza Wideman

For Joelle —DIR

Cedar Crest Books
Natick, MA USA
www.cedarcrestbooks.com

Gwendolyn's Nutty Nutcracker
story by: David Ira Rottenberg
Illustrations by: Zachery Manza Wideman
Copyright © 2018 David Ira Rottenberg

First Printing - April 2019

ISBN: 978-0-910291-22-4

Printed in China by Four Colour Print Group, Louisville, Kentucky
Production Date: November 2018
Batch Number: 82440
Plant Location: GUANGDONG CHINA

Ballet isn't always beautiful.

Gwendolyn feels a little upside down.

The upside—she is dancing in *The Nutcracker*.

The downside—she has never danced in *The Nutcracker* before. Gwendolyn wonders what her role will be....

....Will she be Clara—the girl who receives the magical wooden nutcracker?

Or the Sugar Plum Fairy? Just the name makes Gwendolyn lick her lips in anticipation.

Or will she be the Snow Queen? In her school's ballet, the Snow Queen dances with the Nutcracker Prince.

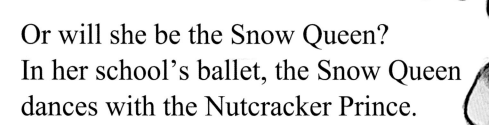

Or, perhaps, she'll be a mouse!
The mice dance a fun part.
They fight the Nutcracker in
a big battle.

Only, Gwendolyn knows mice. The barn is full of mice. They
are very little but very BIG in the *Complaining Department*....

....It's too wet.

It's too cold.

It's too hot.

Gwendolyn does not want to be a mouse.

Lately, the mice grumble to Gwendolyn, "We should play the mice in *The Nutcracker*. *For cheese sake, we are mice!*"

How can Gwendolyn argue with *that?!*
She shrugs...

...and hauls the mice through the snow to the
dance studio. The mice stay warm in the sleigh.

Natasha Levertov, the Artistic Director, studies the mice. They show off, skittering, scurrying, and swaying to *The Nutcracker* music.

"Yes, yes," Natasha sniffs. "I love zheir look,
but zheir legs are veak. Zhey need barre vork."

The mice quickly learn...

...Natasha's word is law.

Omar, Gwendolyn's best friend, trains under
the watchful eye of Bary Mishnakoff.

Bary Mishnakoff and Natasha danced together in Russia.

Under Bary Mishnakoff's patient instruction...

...Omar learns the art of — How to Lift a Ballerina.

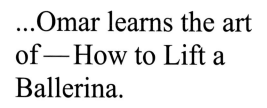

Gwendolyn really, really wants to be the Snow Queen.

Eagerly, she searches through her ballet bag for her new pointe shoes...

...Comb, hairbrush, candy bar, towel, leotard, candy bar, lipstick, candy bar, glue, cell phone, candy bar, bobby pins, scissors, socks, candy bar....

At the bottom of her bag—there they are!

Like every ballerina, Gwendolyn prepares her pointe shoes in her own unique way.

It takes hours of careful work, cutting...

...stretching, pressing, and gluing...

...until they're perfect.

After class, Natasha posts the cast list on the bulletin board.

The students rush to discover their roles.

They react in their usual calm, composed, and dignified manner.

Natasha gathers her students around her. "In ballet, zhere is no such zing as a small part," she says. "Vhenever you are on zhe stage, you are a star."

Alexandra Gomez is Clara.

Rina Rustlehouse is the
Snow Queen.

Aaaaarghhh!!! Imagining Rina Rustlehouse dancing with Omar, Gwendolyn turns green with jealousy.

Natasha comforts Gwendolyn, "Vorking together in harmony—zhat is vhat makes ballet zo beautiful."

Gwendolyn sighs and trudges over to the list.
Her own name is next to a very special
role—The Sugar Plum Fairy!

YES!!!

The night of the performance,
Gwendolyn revels in the part.

She breathes in the bravos down to her toes.

Standing in the wings with Natasha and Bary Mishnakoff, Gwendolyn glares at Omar and Rina. As the two dance, Gwendolyn tries not to make Rina trip with her eyes.

Gwendolyn remembers Natasha's words and mutters to herself, "Harmony, harmony, harmony...."

It works. A little....

Natasha nudges Gwendolyn forward to dance in the Grand Finale.

As Natasha and Bary Mishnakoff watch...

....they think of all the dancers who danced *The Nutcracker* in the past...

...and all the dancers dancing *The Nutcracker* now...

...and all the dancers dancing
The Nutcracker in the future.

As the applause thunders, they join hands with Gwendolyn and Omar and the entire cast. Together, they bow and smile and laugh. The harmony growing in Gwendolyn's heart is so sweet, it almost tickles.

Gwendolyn and Omar dream of next year.
They can't wait to dance with all their friends
in *The Nutcracker* again.